For Lyall. May there never, ever,
EVER be a toad on your head.

In memory of Papa. Every meal in this book
was lovingly prepared just for you.

Tundra Books, an imprint of Penguin Random House Canada Young Readers,
a division of Penguin Random House of Canada Limited

Library and Archives Canada Cataloguing in Publication

Title: Carol and the pickle-toad / Esmé Shapiro.
Names: Shapiro, Esmé, 1992- author, illustrator.
Identifiers: Canadiana (print) 20200211536 | Canadiana (ebook) 20200211544
ISBN 9780735263987 (hardcover) | ISBN 9780735263994 (EPUB)
Classification: LCC PS8637.H3643 C37 2021 | DDC jC813/.6—dc23

Published simultaneously in the United States of America by Tundra Books of
Northern New York, an imprint of Penguin Random House Canada Young Readers,
a division of Penguin Random House of Canada Limited

Library of Congress Control Number: 2020936822

Edited by Tara Walker and Margot Blankier
Designed by John Martz
The artwork in this book was created with watercolor, gouache,
collage, matzo ball soup, colored pencils and a toad.
All paintings were created under quarantine during the pandemic of 2020.
The text was set in Century Schoolbook.

Printed and bound in China

www.penguinrandomhouse.ca

1   2   3   4   5   25   24   23   22   21

Penguin
Random House
TUNDRA BOOKS

CAROL AND THE PICKLE-TOAD

by Esmé Shapiro

tundra

There once lived a girl named Carol who wore a toad as a hat.

Did you know that some people wear toads as hats? Not all, but some do.

Little Shapiro's

50¢ LEMON | hot dog | FREE NOODLE | DELI

OPEN

24 HOURS

HOT DOG | BERRIES

MILK

MUSHROOM | RAVIOLI

HOME MADE

TOAST | YOGURT

Meat 75¢

MIDDLE BEAN | Hello

CAKE | MILK | BREAD

In the big city, people wear all kinds of hats:

big and furry ones,

tall and red ones,

floppy and
wide ones,

and some wear
no hats at all!

But Carol's hat was green,
big-footed and as bossy as
can be.

Carol's toad hat had
opinions on just about
everything!

She would tell her how to bike:

GO THIS WAY!

NO, THAT WAY!

IF I WERE STEERING,
WE WOULD BE THERE
BY NOW!

She would tell Carol what to paint:

NO, NO. THAT'S NO GOOD.
HOW ABOUT ME IN VERY
TALL BOOTS?

And when they went to the deli, she would tell Carol what to eat. Carol's bossy toad was SO loud that everyone would turn and stare.

ONE EGG SANDWICH
WITH A SIDE OF FLIES,
PRONTO!
NO BLINTZES. THEY'RE TOO SQUISHY!

Yes, of all the hats in the big city, Carol's was by far the bossiest AND the rudest. Rudeness, Carol realized, was often a lonely business.

With every day that passed, Carol's voice got quieter and quieter while her bossy toad's grew louder
and
LOUDER.

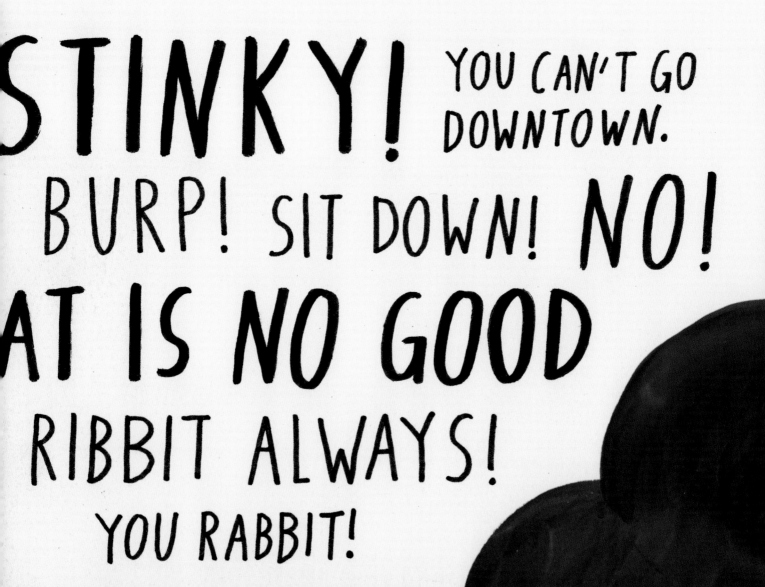

STINKY! YOU CAN'T GO DOWNTOWN.
BURP! SIT DOWN! NO!
AT IS NO GOOD
RIBBIT ALWAYS!
YOU RABBIT!

YOU THINK THAT
TOO MANY BAGELS
YOU ALWAYS EAT
NOOO AN
YOU ARE
RIBBIT
EGG

But you know the old saying, "One never knows when a pigeon may come through your window . . .

and

SCOOP UP
YOUR TOAD HAT!"

With no bossy toad
around, there was no
morning ribbit,

no afternoon ribbit

and no ribbit good night.

Carol tried on other hats.
But none of them made a sound.

She was so used to being bossed
about that she hardly knew what
SHE wanted to do.

She tried to paint, but none
of her brushstrokes felt
quite right.

She tried to bike, but
that certainly didn't
go as planned!

Bonk

Kerplat

SPINK!

At the deli, Carol opened her mouth to order but was too afraid she would get the wrong thing.

So one day the chef just brought her a plate of his choice.

A pickle and an egg . . . ew, how gross! So stinky and shiny.

But then A VISION came to Carol!

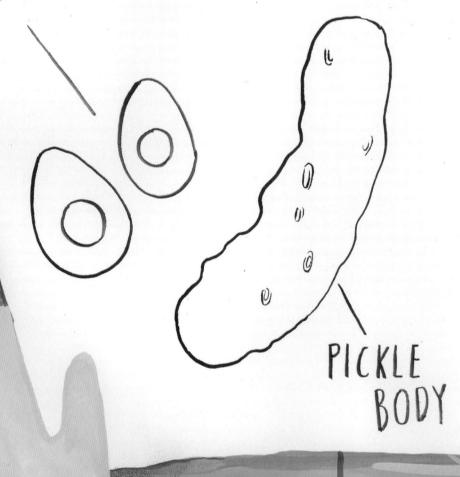

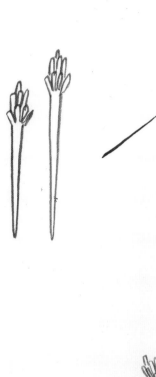

FANCY TOOTHPICKS
TO STICK EVERYTHING
TOGETHER

VOILÀ!

YOU HAVE
YOURSELF A
PICKLE-TOAD!

Did you know some people wear pickle-toads as hats?
Not all, but some do.

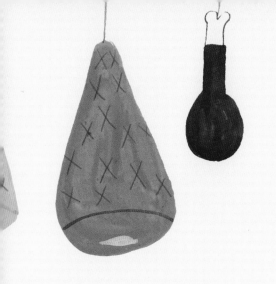
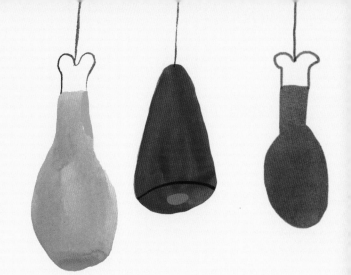

And Carol's pickle-toad hat was the most splendid of them all.

The pickle-toad's voice was quiet, but Carol heard her LOUD.

And with her pickle-toad hat, she ordered all kinds of new things, like matzo ball soup, strawberry shortcake, one latke and three lettuce leaves!

Carol painted all kinds of new things,
not just toads.

Pickle-toad hats are very supportive.

But you know the old saying,
"One never knows when a pigeon
may pass your way . . .

and

SCOOP UP YOUR
PICKLE-TOAD HAT!"

Where oh where
did that pigeon take
Carol's pickle-toad?

She looked
over here and
she looked
over there.

She could not find her pickle-toad hat ANYWHERE!

But then Carol felt something
funny in her tummy.

It felt like it was rumbling.

Then it shook into a roar:

WHERE OH WHERE IS MY PICKLE-TOAD?!!!?

Could it be that this big voice
was in her all along?

Carol leapt into the air and said all kinds of things, like . . .

HELLO!

HOW DO
YOU DO?!

and

YOU LOOK LIKE A BEAUTIFUL BEE!!

Carol found that her voice was quite different
from that of her old toad hat's.

With her big, loud voice everything felt
completely brand-new.

She biked freely, all about town.

With no bossy toad around, she painted
exactly what she liked, thank you very much.

She ordered as many blintzes as she wanted.

BLINTZES FOR MY FRIENDS, PRETTY PLEASE! THE SQUISHIER, THE BETTER!!

Carol realized that kindness was
never a lonely business.

There are many
fabulous voices in
the big city.
But Carol's is the
most wonderful . . .
because it is
all hers.